P9-CAY-263

KIDS CAN'T STOP READING THE CHOOSE YOUR OWN ADVENTURE® STORIES!

"Choose Your Own Adventure is the best thing that has come along since books themselves."
—Alysha Beyer, age 11

"I didn't read much before, but now I read my Choose Your Own Adventure books almost every night."
—Chris Brogan, age 13

"I love the control I have over what happens next."
—Kosta Efstathiou, age 17

"Choose Your Own Adventure books are so much fun to read and collect—I want them all!"
—Brendan Davin, age 11

And teachers like this series, too:
"We have read and reread, worn thin, loved, loaned, bought for others, and donated to school libraries our Choose Your Own Adventure books."

**CHOOSE YOUR OWN ADVENTURE®—
AND MAKE READING MORE FUN!**

Bantam Books in the Choose Your Own Adventure® Series
Ask your bookseller for the books you have missed

FOREST OF FEAR

BY LOUISE MUNRO FOLEY

ILLUSTRATED BY RON WING

An Edward Packard Book

BANTAM BOOKS
TORONTO • NEW YORK • LONDON • SYDNEY • AUCKLAND

RL 4, IL age 10 and up

FOREST OF FEAR
A Bantam Book / March 1986

CHOOSE YOUR OWN ADVENTURE ® *is a registered trademark of
Bantam Books, Inc. Registered in U.S. Patent and Trademark
Office and elsewhere.*

Original conception of Edward Packard

ISBN 0-553-25490-1

Published simultaneously in the United States and Canada

Bantam Books are published by Bantam Books, Inc. Its trademark, consisting of the words "Bantam Books" and the por-
trayal of a rooster, is Registered in U.S. Patent and Trademark
Office and in other countries. Marca Registrada. Bantam
Books, Inc., 666 Fifth Avenue, New York, New York 10103.

PRINTED IN THE UNITED STATES OF AMERICA

0   0 9 8 7 6 5 4 3 2 1

For my son, Don Foley,
who taught me
about confrontation

The threats in our lives are often what save us.

WARNING!!!

Do not read this book straight through from beginning to end. These pages contain many different adventures you may have as you journey through the Forest of Fear. From time to time as you read along you will be asked to make decisions and choices. Your choices may lead to success or disaster.

Your adventures are the result of your choices. *You* are responsible because *you* choose! After you make your choice, follow the instructions to see what happens next.

Think carefully before you make a move. You may find yourself in other times and other realms. Will you ever find your way out of the Forest of Fear? It's up to you!

Good luck!

When your mother's company sends her to France for the summer, her younger brother—your uncle Jason—invites you to stay with him. Jason lives in an abandoned ranger station in a forest in northeastern Maine. He bought the lookout years ago and supports himself by writing adventure novels. You still remember the fun you had when you were small, and imaginative, easygoing Jason came to visit. You're eager to go. You love to hike, and you're sure Jason will help you explore the best trails.

The day after school is out you board a bus for Maine. For the last fifty miles your seatmate is an old man named Isaac Cairns. You learn that Isaac lives about six miles from Jason.

"Have you lived around here all your life?" you ask him.

"Yup," he replies. "All seventy years of it. Only the Indians know these forest better'n Isaac Cairns. When I was your age, my best friend was a Penobscot. Henry Madokawando and I grew up together in the forest. My family homesteaded here."

When you tell him where you're going, he scowls.

Turn to page 2.

"Never should have pulled the ranger out of that station," he mutters. "They'll regret it this summer, mark my words."

"You mean, there'll be a forest fire?" you ask.

"Yup, a ripsnorter. A crown fire will take out all the pines on the southwest slope."

"How do you know that?" you ask.

"It's been hot and dry. Not much snow runoff from last winter," he snaps. "City folk ain't got no heads for nature's mischief. If I had my way, they'd shoot any stranger who goes beyond Wolf Ridge."

At that Isaac pulls his hat over his eyes and starts to snore.

Turn to page 5.

"I'll help," Mrs. Ellison says, joining you at the woodpile. "They'll be here soon."

"But they're not coming till closing time," you tell her.

Mrs. Ellison smiles. "When people are motivated by easy money, they become impatient."

Sure enough, as Mrs. Ellison stacks the last log, you look up to see Stan and Fred coming from the forest.

"Where's the shotgun?" you ask.

"I hid it. It would only cause problems," she whispers. "What can I do for you?" she says to the men as they approach.

"Get inside," Stan snaps, grabbing her arm. Fred shoves you inside after them. "Now open the cash register!" Stan orders.

Mrs. Ellison pushes the NO SALE key. The drawer opens.

"Empty!" Stan yells. "Where's the money?"

"I hid it under the woodpile," she tells him calmly. "I knew you were coming. Your conversation in the cabin was overheard."

"Sit on the step," he snaps, pushing her back outside.

Mrs. Ellison motions for you to sit beside her.

"This'll take forever!" Fred yells, swinging a piece of wood. "Make them help too!"

Just what you wanted to hear! With a piece of wood in your hands you may be able to knock one of them out.

"And give them a chance to swing logs at us?" Stan growls at Fred. "We'll do it alone."

Turn to page 111.

When the bus pulls up at Ellison's Store, Jason, wearing blue jeans and a flannel shirt, is waiting. He has a beard now, you notice, but somehow doesn't look much older than when you last saw him. He points to his dirt bike, parked by the gas pump. "Hop on," he says.

You ride to the ranger station through dense forest. At last you see the lookout—Jason's home— towering over hundreds of acres of spruce and pines.

Turn to page 7.

"This way," you say, turning left into the forest.

"Who's this Henry fellow?" Fred says, puffing along behind you. "And what's so special about this tree?"

"I'll tell you the story," you say, turning to hide your smile. You wondered how long it would be before they'd ask.

"What happened to the Indian who took a piece of the bark?" Stan asks when you finish the story.

"He was able to predict the future," you say.

"Lucky dog," Stan mutters. "I'd like to know what's in my future. Like if we're going to outwit those Boston cops."

"Go buy a crystal ball," Fred grunts. "How much farther?"

"Not far," you say confidently. But inside you're worrying. The sky is darkening quickly—there may be a storm coming in. And that's the least of your problems. How much longer can you lie to them and get away with it? Will they guess that you really don't know where the tree is?

Turn to page 9.

"Are there any other people around?" you ask, following Jason up the ladderlike stairs that lead to the glass-walled lookout.

"Nope," says Jason. "Closest is Agnes Ellison at the store."

He opens the door and you enter. "That's your room," he says, pointing to one screened-off corner. He points to another screen and says, "This one's mine."

There are cots behind each of the screens; a sink without taps; and a two-burner stove. An old couch is in the center of the room, and Jason's typewriter is set up on a card table. Beside it sits a fancy two-way radio and a pair of binoculars.

"My link to the world," Jason says, nodding at the radio.

You walk around the table and look at the page in the typewriter. "Is this your new book? Can I read it?"

"Not now," he says. "It's bad luck to show a partial manuscript to anyone. You can read it when it's finished."

"Okay," you say, but your heart is thumping. The single paragraph you read is astonishing:

A crown fire will take out all the pines on the southwest slope. It's been hot and dry. Not much snow runoff from last winter.

Isaac Cairn's words! But Jason wrote this before you arrived!

"You can read it when it's finished," Jason repeats firmly. "Get unpacked. I'm going down for some water."

Turn to page 12.

8

"It's crazy to cross that gorge," you tell the Indian boy. "Go alone!"

You raise your arms and with both hands toss the sapling out over the gorge. Slim and flexible, it quivers horizontally for a split second like a vibrating violin string, then tips and falls like an arrow to the bottom of the abyss.

You look to the Indian boy, now halfway across the gorge, the pine log rolling treacherously under his feet as he struggles to keep his balance. There is no sign of life on the other side, no indication that a shaman with bow and arrow waits to exact a coward's penalty.

Turn to page 61.

You crawl through a stand of second growth. Charred logs indicate a previous fire, and you think of Mrs. Ellison's warning. Your imagination is so active, you even think you can smell smoke.

"Is that it?" Fred yells, pointing.

In the middle of a small clearing is a pine tree. You can't stall them any longer. You nod. "That's it."

"Okay," says Stan. "Where's the cash drawer?"

"Over there," you lie, pointing to the back of the tree.

"Start digging, Fred," Stan says, walking up to the tree. He reaches up and touches a cone hanging from one bough.

Fred starts pawing through the soft earth. Stan circles the tree, viewing it from every angle. When both are preoccupied, you start backing away. Then Stan turns around and sees you. With a roar he lunges toward you.

Turn to page 96.

"I was very worried," Jason says, squatting down beside you. "Come on, let's go home."

"Yes. Come and have some rabbit stew with me," you say. You head toward the cabin.

"What are you talking about?" Jason asks as you lead him inside.

"I have it on the stove," you say.

"But there is no stove," Jason replies. "This cabin was burned out a hundred year ago."

By the time Jason gets you back to the ranger station, you have no interest in doing anything. You don't want to read or talk. You just want to go back to the cabin. In desperation Jason padlocks the door to keep you from leaving the lookout. The next day he takes you to a doctor, but even medication doesn't improve your condition.

Eventually you're sent back to the city and placed in an institution. You spend the rest of your life sketching pictures of a stunted, misshapen pine tree. You tell everyone who looks at your artwork that it is the Spirit Tree. And occasionally, when you're in the cafeteria, you ask the workers for a bowl of Sarah's rabbit stew.

The End

You give Jason enough time to get to the ground and then hurry back to the typewriter. There's nothing else on the page you read, so you flip through those on the table. As you do you notice the name *Isaac* in several places. At last you come to page one. The title reads *The Spirit Tree,* and beside it Jason has sketched a pine tree. You start to read:

Deep in the forest there was a pine tree that remained the same from year to year and season to season. Despite fires and floods that devastated the rest of the forest, this tree was never destroyed. The Indians believed that the tree could give them supernatural powers—power to see into the future and power to travel into the past—for it was the way station for spirits, both evil and good. Hovering in its upper branches, the spirits waited patiently until the time was right to possess the bodies of those who kept vigil or passed in its shadow.

Because of its sacred nature this one tree was never to be disturbed. No pinecones could be picked, no branches cut. Elders of the tribe often consulted the tree when seeking answers to problems, and young Indian men were required to sit alone in its shadow on the night before they were to become braves.

Go on to the next page.

However, one young man, who was in contention with his cousin to follow their uncle as chief of the tribe, was not satisfied to sit in the tree's shadow.

"If the tree's shadow can bestow on me the gift of past and future," he reasoned, "surely a piece of the bark carefully stitched into my moccasin would give me even greater power." He reached up with a sharp rock and cut off a piece of the bark. . . .

You hear a noise and quickly stop reading.

Turn to page 44.

"Benjamin!" Sarah says. "The shoes and clothes of our guest are oddities, but remember, Pa used to say that what we are does not show on the outside. We cannot know someone by their garb."

"Hush, sister," Ben snaps. "Have you forgotten something else Pa told us? About the tree?"

"Do you know where the tree is?" you ask impatiently.

"Yes," Ben replies. He picks up his knife from the table.

"You must not go there, Benjamin!" Sarah says sharply. "We promised Pa we would not go to the tree! It is dangerous!"

"I am not going there!" Ben stands up so quickly that he rocks the table. "I am answering our guest's question." He turns to you. "I will escort you to the top of the ridge. Come."

It is more of an order than an invitation. Hesitantly you follow him outside. Dusk is already closing in.

Go on to the next page.

"Come," Ben repeats, running his thumb over the blade of the knife. "I will lead you where you want to go."

"To the tree?" you ask. "Have you been there?"

"Yes," he replies curtly. "Have you?"

You stare at him, puzzled, and then blurt out, "No!"

"Do you lie?" he asks, gripping the knife handle tightly.

"No!" you say. "I haven't been there! But I want to know about it. And about spirit possession. What is it?"

"Do not ask me that question," he says through tight lips. "Do you wish to go to the tree?"

*If you say yes and go with Ben,
turn to page 38.*

If you decide not to go, turn to page 46.

You jump up and hurry in the direction of the wolves. Their howls grow louder as you approach the top of the ridge, and when you break through the trees, you see a terrifying sight. Ben is on the ground, and around him are circling not one but four wolves.

If you only had a weapon! But the only weapon available is Ben's knife, shimmering uselessly in the moonlight beside him. You must do something right away! you tell yourself. Your hand goes to the camera hanging about your neck. You creep in as close as you dare. One of the wolves senses your presence and turns. Now! You push the shutter and the flash glares into the night. The wolf backs away. Again and again and again you push the shutter as the flashcube spins around in its socket.

With a howl one wolf runs for the woods. Another follows and another until the pack is gone. Quickly you run to Ben.

"I caught my foot on a root. Twisted my ankle," he gasps. "They moved in like lightning." He reaches for your hand and then backs away from the camera, which is swinging from around your neck.

"It won't hurt you," you assure him, helping him up.

Turn to page 20.

"You want to visit the Spirit Tree," the man says, ignoring your question.

"How did you know that?" you ask, backing away.

"I know," he says.

"Are you Henry?"

He nods. "Come. I will take you."

"I do want to see the tree, but not now!" you say quickly. "Mrs. Ellison is in danger. You must show me the way back."

"I cannot do that," Henry says, shaking his head. "Each one has his own trail to find."

You jump up. "But you don't understand! There are two convicts—"

"I understand," Henry says. "You may come or return."

You look overhead through the heavy branches. Little light sifts through. You're sure you've been wandering for hours. You don't know what time it is, but it must be past six. You may not be much help to Mrs. Ellison now.

If you go with Henry, turn to page 29.

If you try to find the store, turn to page 54.

"Henry hasn't been at the cabin for over a year!" Mrs. Ellison mutters. "He went back to the forest."

"Please call the police," you plead.

"Can't do that," she says. "Line got struck by lightning the other night. Bus driver said he'd report it to the phone company, but I guess he forgot." She walks to the back of the store and returns carrying a shotgun. "I'll just have to handle this myself. If this can stop a black bear, it can stop a couple of crooks," she says. "Now, are you going to help me with that wood or aren't you? I can't gab all day."

You think hard. You hate to leave Mrs. Ellison alone with two convicts on the loose. But if you go back to the lookout, Jason can radio for help. Of course, if you leave, you'll risk meeting the convicts in the forest.

*If you decide to stay with Mrs. Ellison,
turn to page 88.*

*If you go back through the forest,
turn to page 32.*

By the time you get Ben back to the cabin, you're exhausted. Sarah pulls a straw pallet down from the loft, and you curl up in a corner of the kitchen near the door. In the morning you're awakened by voices. Bone-weary and cold, you open your eyes. Jason is leaning over you. Overhead the sun is streaming into the room. The cabin is nothing but a burned-out shell!

"Where are Ben and Sarah?" you ask.

"Don't talk now," he tells you. "You've had a rough night. I should never have let you go off alone."

Turn to page 52.

Later that night when you go to bed, you're still wondering how Jason knew exactly what Isaac said to you on the bus. Is Jason psychic? Could it have something to do with the powers of the Spirit Tree?

You're sure something strange is going on. Jason's so crabby; it's as if he's turned into another person. Maybe you should find Henry and ask him about the tree. And how does the legend end? you wonder. Henry could tell you.

Your other choice is to sneak back to the table and try to read the rest of the story now.

If you decide to find Henry in the morning, turn to page 51.

If you decide to try to finish reading the story now, turn to page 73.

You unwrap your sandwiches and eat them, staring at the trees along the ridge, trying to match one with Jason's sketch. The sun is warm and the air is humid, and you're sleepy.

The low, threatening grumble of thunder wakens you. At first you can't remember where you are. But there's one thing you do remember: Don't sit under a tree during a thunderstorm!

Lightning flashes against the dark sky, and you jump up and run. Rain comes down in huge drops, and you race down the other side of the ridge, looking for cover. Ahead of you is a deep canyon. Behind you is a forest of tall trees, many of them already scarred by lightning strikes. You slip on the needle-covered ground, panicking when you lose your balance. You plummet down the sharp angle of the cliff, stopping only when you crash into a boulder. You grab hold of a bush and watch as the huge rock bounces downhill, gathering small rocks in its path.

Turn to page 24.

24

That's when you see it. Off to the right, within easy crawling distance, is the covered bridge! If you can reach that, you'll be safe from the storm. It spans a deep, narrow gorge—so deep that you can't see the bottom. Jason's warning rings in your ears. But the rain is pounding on you and the lightning is coming closer.

The downpour is dislodging other boulders from the side of the ridge. You don't want to be caught in a rockslide!

You crawl the short distance to the bridge and enter its dark tunnel.

Turn to page 114.

Quietly you back down the steps. The shotgun is still leaning against the building. You grab it and hurry into the trees. But you can't remember where you hid the cash drawer. You run from one tree to another, pushing the brush aside, but you can't find the hiding place! Loud voices interrupt your search.

"I'll tell you nothing until you take your hands off me!" Mrs. Ellison says. The men are bringing her down the steps.

Quickly you conceal the shotgun under a bush. Using it would be foolish, you tell yourself. You couldn't fire without endangering Mrs. Ellison, and you don't want the convicts to get hold of it!

She shakes free of their grasp. "The cash drawer is in the woodpile," she says. "At the bottom."

"If it's not in here, lady, you're in trouble," Stan says.

Your heart skips a beat. You're the only one who knows it's *not* in there! You watch as the men start dismantling the wood pile. You must find the cash drawer before they get to the bottom. You crawl from tree to tree, looking without success. Stan's angry voice finally stops your search.

"You lied, lady! There's nothing here! No money!"

He moves menacingly toward Mrs. Ellison.

"Leave her alone!" you yell, running out of the forest. "She didn't lie. She thought it was there. I moved it! I hid it in the forest while she was inside fixing lunch."

Turn to page 37.

"Thank you," you say. "I'd like to stay for dinner."

You follow them into the cabin. A pot is simmering on the old-fashioned stove, and a pine table has been set for dinner.

"You're lucky! It's rabbit stew," Sarah says, bringing the pot to the table. Your stomach shifts uneasily. "Ben's been tryin' for days to catch us a rabbit. Most of the small animals have gone to the forest's edge. The drought has dried up their food."

"How long have you lived here?" you ask hesitantly.

"We were born here," Ben says. "Pa was born here too. Well, not in this cabin, but in the forest. He was part Indian. Pa knew every tree and every hollow. Taught me lots too."

"We tried to save Ma and Pa when they got sick," Sarah says. "Ben brought me the medicine man's herbs and roots. But the sickness was too far along."

You poke at the stew in your dish and wonder what you should say or do next. This is all unbelievable! How could these people from Jason's book have come to life? How could you have wandered into another period of time? A thought suddenly occurs to you. Since Ben and Sarah and the Spirit Tree are all in Jason's book, maybe they know something about it.

Go on to the next page.

"Did your father or Isaac ever talk about a special tree around here?" you ask. "One that the Indians thought was sacred?"

Benjamin and Sarah exchange glances.

"Why have you come here, stranger?" Ben asks, his voice suddenly cold. He wipes his mouth with the back of his hand. "Who are you? You are not the preacher's kin. You wear strange clothing, and you ask impertinent questions."

Turn to page 14.

"I'll come," you say to Henry, following him into the forest.

You walk a long time without speaking, but your mind is full of questions. Finally you break the silence.

"Tell me about your tree," you say. "Are we almost there?"

"Yes," Henry replies. He stoops down and crawls through a low stand of bushes, exiting in a small clearing.

"This is the Spirit Tree," he says softly.

Henry sits cross-legged on the forest floor in front of a small pine, and hesitantly you sit beside him. Overhead the evening sky shows both a setting sun, in warm reds and yellows—and a rising moon, suspended in deep purple. It is as though time has stopped—as if the powers of nature have become confused, and something supernatural is taking place.

"Do the spirits of dead people really live in its branches?" you whisper, shivering at the thought.

Henry nods. "Both good and evil spirits," he replies.

"Isn't it risky to sit here?" you ask, uncomfortable with the strange silence of the forest.

"All life is a risk," he replies. "One must respect the gift of life and accept what comes with it, good and bad."

"I want to go back," you say, turning to Henry.

But Henry has disappeared!

Turn to page 48.

After breakfast Jason gruffly tells you to do the dishes while he goes down to get more water.

As soon as he leaves you get the pages from under the blanket and put them back on the card table. You glance again quickly at the page with the story of the Spirit Tree. What could be so dangerous about a tree? The two penciled words jump out at you again. *Spirit possession.* It's just a story. Or is it? There's only one way to find out.

"I think I'll go hiking," you tell Jason when he returns.

"Pack some sandwiches," he grunts, sitting down at the typewriter. "You'll have to amuse yourself. I can't go. I have to finish this book. I'm not going to be much company for you."

"That's okay," you tell him. "I'll just wander."

Unexpectedly Jason grins. "You'd better not 'just wander,'" he says. "You could wander yourself right into trouble. There are two fairly safe trails from the lookout. The one to the left goes into the meadow. There's a burned-out log cabin down there, and you may find some arrowheads along the creek. The other," he continues, pointing through the doorway, "goes up to Wolf Ridge."

*If you choose the trail to the meadow,
turn to page 92.*

*If you choose the trail to the ridge,
turn to page 33.*

"No," you reply. "Stay put. Don't you remember? I told you the Spirit Tree never changes. Not in drought or winter or fire."

You hope, as you speak, that the legend is true, because it's no longer just a story, but a matter of life and death. Crackling noises like gunshots fill the air as the dry timber surrounding you goes up in flames. You're sure that at any minute a flaming tree will land on you.

"I hear a plane," Fred mumbles, without raising his head.

You listen carefully. It's too dark now for an aerial search, you think. Still, you do hear something above the roar of the flames.

Hours after the borate bombers have put out the blaze Jason and a rescue team find you and Fred. Dawn is breaking as they carry you out, and you look back at the Spirit Tree. Firmly centered in the middle of a ring of charred earth, it is standing unchanged.

"Did you find Stan?" Fred asks Jason.

Jason nods. "He got trapped on the slope," he says quietly.

After Fred has been taken into custody and you're safely back in the ranger station, you curl up on the couch and watch Jason as he fixes you something to eat.

"You know, it's actually good luck to let people read unfinished manuscripts," you say slowly. "If I hadn't read that the tree never changed, I'd be dead."

The End

"I'm going back to have Jason radio for help,"
you tell Mrs. Ellison. "I'll double-back through the
forest."

"Humph," Mrs. Ellison snorts. "Don't get lost.
Even the Indians had to mark trails, you know."

"I won't get lost," you reply indignantly.

You leave the store and hurry into the forest.
You must get to Jason quickly. You look up
through the trees, trying to spot the lookout tower,
but the overhead branches are too thick. You walk
for a long time. Suddenly you realize that you're
lost! Several times you change direction. Everything looks the same—you can't tell if you're re-
tracing your steps or going farther into the forest.
And it's getting dark. You sit on a rock to think.

You're so caught up in your concentration that
at first you don't see the man. His clothing blends
with the surroundings as he stands motionless at
the edge of the small clearing, watching you.

You look up and open your mouth to speak, but
fear blocks the words. He starts moving silently
toward you, his eyes fixed sternly on your face.

"I'm lost," you say. The words come out in a
croak.

He nods his head and stops just a few feet away.
His gray hair is long and his tan face is grooved
with deep lines. Yet his carriage is erect, and you
sense his quiet strength.

"All of us are lost," he says in a voice much
gentler than his appearance.

"Who are you?" you ask.

Turn to page 18.

"I guess I'll go up to Wolf Ridge," you tell Jason. There's not much chance the tree will be in the meadow, you think.

"Well, stay on the trail," he snaps. "And keep away from the covered bridge. It's not safe."

A warning signal flashes in your mind. Is the bridge really unsafe, or is Jason trying to steer you away from the Spirit Tree? Maybe the tree is on the other side of the bridge. Or maybe the tree is just a product of Jason's imagination. But why would he lie to you?

"And don't waste your time looking for the Spirit Tree," he continues. "It doesn't exist. I made it up."

Startled, you look at him without replying. How did he know what you were thinking?

You jab a knife into a jar of peanut butter and start making sandwiches. Jason turns back to his writing. Neither of you speaks again until you're on your way out.

"Stay away from the bridge," Jason calls as the door bangs behind you.

As you climb the grade to the ridge you try to imagine what has changed Jason, and what happened to the young Indian in his story. Maybe the spirits of the tree possessed him when he cut away the bark. Maybe he died right there, before his night in its shadow was over. Or maybe he became chief, honored by all the tribes in the area, because he could predict the future. . . .

You reach the top of the ridge and sit down to rest.

Turn to page 22.

Suddenly you are grabbed from behind. "My sister said not to point that thing at her," says the young man holding you. The tip of a razor-sharp hunting knife rests on your throat.

"It won't hurt her!" you say. "Who are you?"

"Benjamin Scott," the young man replies.

Your mind leaps back to Jason's book. "And your sister is Sarah," you say, in a choked voice.

"How did you know that?" Benjamin asks, loosening his grip.

"Oh! You must be kin to the preacher!" Sarah exclaims. "Let go, Ben!" She hurries over to you. "You're our first visitor in a month! No one will come near since the sickness was here. We were lucky the preacher came this way. He gave Ma and Pa a decent burial."

Ben frowns. "That's right. The preacher said he had kin in the area." He stretches out his hand. "We welcome you. You'll be stayin' the night with us then, and go on in the morning."

"Well, no, I . . ." You start to say you're not kin to any preacher and then stop. "I can't stay," you tell them. "I must get back to the ranger station before dark."

Turn to page 36.

Sarah frowns at you. "Ranger station? What ye be talkin' about? You'll scarcely get to the top of the next ridge before dark. The wolves out there are mean. The drought has left them with slim pickin's."

You look to the top of the ridge. The sun is already dipping in the sky. Can you have spent that much time in the forest? Have you truly stumbled into another century?

"Our evening meal is fixed," Ben says. "Come share it."

If you decide to stay, turn to page 26.

If you decide to leave, turn to page 78.

"The forest's a big place, kid," says Stan. "Where did you hide the cash drawer?"

Mrs. Ellison looks at you, puzzled.

Your mind is racing a mile a minute. You got Mrs. Ellison into this mess. You're going to have to get her out of it. You'd better think up a good story.

You scowl at Stan. "I'll take you to it, but only if you leave Mrs. Ellison here. She's too old to crawl through the forest."

Mrs. Ellison gives you a disgusted look.

"Sure," says Stan sarcastically. "Leave her here to call the cops!"

"The phone's out of order," you say. "And no customers are going to come by. Everybody's at the River Race."

Stan looks at Fred. "She will slow us down."

He turns back to you. "Okay, but tell me where it's hidden."

"I hid it under Henry's tree," you say slowly.

Mrs. Ellison's eyes flicker as they meet yours. "There's a fire alert posted for the ridge," she says.

Is she trying to tell you that the Spirit Tree is at the ridge? That she wants you to go there?

"Who's Henry?" Stan asks suspiciously.

"An Indian who used to live around here," you tell him. "His tree is sacred. It has special powers."

"Death waits for you by Henry's tree," Mrs. Ellison says to Stan, looking him in the eye.

"Don't try to scare us away from the money!" Stan snaps.

Mrs. Ellison looks at you. "The writing's on the wall," she says mysteriously.

Turn to page 67.

"Yes," you say to Ben. "Take me to the tree."

He veers to the right and leads you into dense shadowy forest. A wolf is howling in the distance. Suddenly Ben stops.

"The tree is there," he says, waving his hand ahead of him.

"But there are dozens of trees there!" you snap. "Which one?"

"By morning you will know," he replies. "Good-bye."

"Wait!" you yell, grabbing his arm. "Why was Sarah afraid of the tree?"

He pulls out of your grasp and faces you, his eyes full of fear. "The tree is the dwelling place of the dead," he says, his voice cracking as he speaks. "Spirits—good and evil—wait in its branches to possess the souls of those who come near."

"You mean, I could become someone else?" you ask.

"What we are does not show on the outside," he says, backing away into the forest.

"Wait!" you yell, but your cry is drowned out by the cry of a wolf. You circle several majestic pines, looking for Ben, but he has disappeared. And night has come to the forest.

Go on to the next page.

"Stay calm," you tell yourself, but your knees are shaking. You sit down by a small misshapen pine, dwarfed by the towering trees around it.

A thought occurs to you. What if Ben and Sarah are possessed by spirits? You must get out of here! The tree is dangerous. You've got to avoid it, but you don't even know which one it is! The cries of the wolves grow louder, and between the howls you hear a human cry! Could the wolves have trapped Ben on the ridge? Should you go and check?

If you go toward the wolves, turn to page 17.

If you try to find your way back to the ranger station, turn to page 64.

You're put into a private room. Someone takes a sample of your blood and several doctors examine you. You're not fully conscious of who is in the room, but despite your fever, you recognize Jason's voice. He's talking to one of the doctors.

"I find it hard to believe," the doctor whispers,

"but you're right! The child has cholera. There hasn't been a case in the area for a hundred years."

Go on to the next page.

On the day you're released from the hospital Jason takes you back to the lookout.

"Is cholera what killed Ben and Sarah's parents?" you ask him.

He nods.

"Did I get it from Ben and Sarah?"

"No," he says, "you got it from the water in the barrel."

"How do you know? And how did you know about Ben and Sarah?" You hesitate. "Jason, have you been to the tree?"

"No," he says, gently. He picks up a musty, leatherbound book. "It's all recorded here in this history of the area. These facts were the basis for my story. Shortly after Mr. and Mrs. Scott died, a young stranger—kin of a preacher—visited Sarah and Ben. The stranger contracted cholera."

"And I was the stranger," you say, already knowing the answer. "But that doesn't explain how I walked into another century! Where did Ben and Sarah come from? And where did they go?"

"There's only one way to explain that," Jason says.

You look at him and shiver.

Turn to page 112.

You open the cabin door and run back to the ranger station.

"What's up?" Jason asks, irritated at the interruption.

You quickly tell him about the escaped convicts. His face grows pale and his eyes cloud with fear.

"They didn't see me," you assure him, puzzled at his fright. "And they're not coming here. Just radio for the police."

He nods and switches on the set, but his hand trembles.

By early afternoon the police have picked up the escaped convicts at the cabin. You and Jason watch through binoculars.

"You'll have to tell Henry about it," you say.

"Henry disappeared a year ago," Jason says quietly.

"Where did he go?" you ask.

"I think he went to the tree," Jason says.

"Do you know where it is?"

"Don't ask me that!" he snaps. He rips the page from his typewriter and throws it in the trash. "I can't write with you jabbering. I'm going for a walk." The door slams after him.

Turn to page 113.

It's Jason, coming back with the water. You set the page down, but you're not quick enough.

"Do you want to jinx this book for me?" Jason asks, annoyed.

"No!" you say. "But I had to read more. You see, you wrote down exactly what a man said to me on the bus."

Jason's dark brows furrow. "Show me," he says.

"There!" You point to the page in the typewriter. "You even knew Isaac's name! It's almost as if you have some psychic power!"

Jason shrugs. "Coincidence. I know Isaac Cairns. I just borrowed his name for the book. His father and his grandfather had the same name. And with so little snow runoff from last winter, the natives of this area all know the fire danger."

"Will you tell me about the Spirit Tree?" you ask.

Jason looks at you, irritated. "Did you read the whole thing?"

"No," you say. "Just some of it. Did you make it up?"

"The tree? Good heavens, no! I heard it from Henry Madokawando, an old Indian who has a cabin out by the road."

"Henry used to be a friend of Isaac Cairns!" you say. "Did he tell you the ending? What happened to the young Indian?"

"Forget the tree!" Jason snaps. "It's dangerous!"

Turn to page 21.

Puzzled, you go into Mrs. Ellison's living room and open the damper in the fireplace.

"Now, go watch, and tell me when they get to the bottom of the woodpile. I'll have to discourage them from coming back in here."

You squat at the window, watching. When the men get down to the last layer of logs, you call out, "They're at the bottom! And they're heading for the store!"

"Plug your ears," she says. She sits on the hearth and blasts the shotgun up the chimney.

"They're going!" you yell. "And they're stealing Jason's bike! You've got the gun! Stop them!"

"Don't worry," Mrs. Ellison says. "The police will stop them. In fact, I told Stan where to find Jason's bike. I knew Jason would radio the police as soon as it was stolen. They won't go far."

"You sent them to steal Jason's bike?" you ask.

"Of course. Jason bought two dollars' worth of gas on Monday," she explains patiently. "By now there can't be much left in the tank. They'll get just far enough down the road to keep them out of our hair before they run out of gas. The police will pick them up before they can walk back. So we're safe."

"You're pretty smart," you say.

"You have to keep your wits about you if you live in this forest," Mrs. Ellison says. "You can't just go around looking for trees with special powers." She puts down the shotgun and heads for the door. "Come on," she continues. "We've got a cord of wood to stack before dark."

The End

"No," you say, eyeing Benjamin's knife. "I don't want to go to the tree."

"Then leave, and do not return," he says. He turns and walks quickly back down the ridge. You watch him walk behind the cabin and then hurry into the forest.

When you reach the tower, you climb the ladder quickly. Jason meets you at the doorway. "Where have you been?" he demands.

Quickly you tell him about Benjamin and Sarah.

"They're in your book," you say. "How did you know about them?"

Turn to page 53.

You jump to your feet and pivot in a circle as you peer into the trees, trying to see where Henry went. But there is no sign of him. None!

You glance at the sky. The glow of the sunset is almost gone, and the silver moon hangs in a black sky. Above you the dark branches of the Spirit Tree move slightly in the night breeze.

You sit down and try to think through your plight logically.

You can spend the night in the clearing by the tree, or you can try to find your way back to the lookout. The latter seems to be an impossibility. You've traveled miles since you left the store. Walking through the forest at night just doesn't seem sensible. But sitting here under the Spirit Tree isn't very comforting.

On the other hand the story *is* a legend. It isn't fact. It's a tale that superstitious people from years ago recounted from one generation to the next. And the story probably got better with each telling, just like gossip.

The fact is, dead people are dead, you tell yourself. They don't sit in branches of trees, waiting to enter someone else's body.

If you continue your search for the lookout tower, turn to page 102.

If you spend the night by the Spirit Tree, turn to page 74.

"Five minutes is plenty of time," you reply coolly. But your heart is pounding. Will there be enough time for you to get out of sight?

You head for the ridge on the run. If only there were a hollow or a heavily overgrown section where you could double-back! But the slope to the ridge angles up so you are visible as you climb. A flash of lightning is closely followed by the ominous rumble of thunder. You start to run. No point in pretending any longer. If you're going to escape them, you're going to have to go down the other side of the ridge.

You glance back. Fred and Stan are lumbering up the ridge behind you, but you have a good head start. Hoping there will be a trail leading down the other side, you veer to the left and stop. Squatting in a ring of trees is a small pine tree— exactly like Henry's drawing! Spellbound, you circle it.

A bolt of lightning spears the tops of the trees near you, and you look up in alarm. A lazy curl of smoke is rising from the crown of a dead tree just north of the clearing. As you watch, the tree leans sideways. If it should fall into the stand of pines, the whole ridge will ignite! you realize. You look back. Fred and Stan are getting close. Should you warn them? Or run?

If you decide to warn them, turn to page 82.

If you decide to run, turn to page 98.

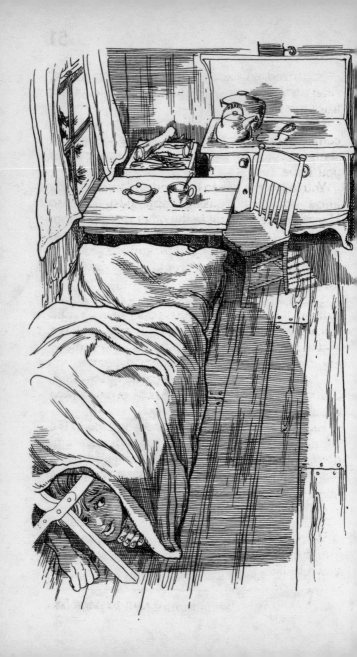

You need an excuse to go to Henry's cabin. After breakfast you ask Jason if he needs anything from the store.

"Yes," he says. "See if my typing paper has come in. And get the mail." He sits down and starts to type. "Turn right at the road," he calls as you leave.

You follow the trail to the road and turn left. You know you didn't pass a cabin yesterday, so Henry's place must be in the other direction from the store. You walk a long time before you come to a small wooden building. It looks deserted.

"Anybody home?" you yell. "Henry, are you in there?"

You push open the door. There's no one inside. But on the wall across the room the sunlight catches a drawing. Burned into the soft wood is a sketch of a pine tree. It's exactly like Jason's drawing of the Spirit Tree, only larger. You enter.

The single-room shack is sparsely furnished. Something tells you that it has not been occupied for a long time. Where is Henry?

Feeling like a criminal, you move quietly to the etching of the tree. The natural knotholes and grain of the unfinished wall boards add to its beauty. Did Henry do the etching? you wonder. Does this tree really exist?

A noise outside startles you.

"Hello. Anybody in there?" a voice shouts.

Who is it? What if you're caught trespassing? You duck under the cot and pull the gray blanket down to hide you.

Turn to page 58.

When you're safely back at the tower, you tell Jason about your adventure. "Do you believe me?" you ask hesitantly.

"Yes," he says solemnly. "Henry has told me of similar excursions into the past. They were always connected with his visits to the tree."

"But I didn't visit the tree! I was afraid! I got back to the ridge as fast as I could. The only tree I sat by was a runt—a scrawny, lopsided dwarf. It wasn't at all like your sketch."

"But I've never seen the Spirit Tree," Jason says. "The sketch came from my imagination."

"Well, I didn't imagine what happened last night," you declare.

"I believe you," he says. "Maybe it's the same with trees as with people. What they are doesn't show on the outside."

The End

Jason sighs. "Sit down," he says gently, motioning you to the couch. "Before Henry disappeared, he told me a story about the Spirit Tree. A story about a family who lived in the forest a hundred years ago. . . ."

He looks into your questioning eyes and nods.

"The Scotts," he continues. "The mother and father died of cholera. Sarah and Ben were spared and lived in the log cabin for a few years after the death of their parents."

"Just a few years?" you ask.

Jason nods. "Yes," he says.

"What happened to them?"

"One summer night during a freak storm, the cabin was hit by lightning. Sarah and Ben were asleep in the loft. The wood was tinder-dry. They didn't have a chance to get out. Sarah and Ben died in the fire. The tragedy was discovered by a traveling preacher who was on his way through the forest."

"The preacher!" you say. "They talked about the preacher!"

Jason nods. "It all happened," he says solemnly.

Turn to page 100.

"I can't go to the tree now," you tell Henry.

With a slight nod of his head he moves into the trees and vanishes as quickly as he appeared.

You turn around and start walking. Your mind is in turmoil. What if you can't find your way out? Was Mrs. Ellison robbed by the convicts? Maybe murdered? What if you meet a black bear?

No sooner has the thought of a wild animal crossed your mind than you hear rustling in the bushes to your right.

You look frantically around for a place to hide. The trees are all too tall to climb. You dive into a patch of brush and huddle down, trying to make yourself as small as possible.

Whatever it is, it's coming close. And it's big!

You look around for a rock, but there are none within reach. Desperate, you settle for a clump of dirt. Just as the creature breaks through the bushes, you raise your arm and let the clump of dirt fly.

"Fine way to treat a rescuer!" sputters a voice.

Isaac Cairns comes into view, shaking the dirt from his head and neck.

"You have good aim. I'll give you that," he says grudgingly. "Come on, let's go back before it gets black as pitch."

"I'm sorry," you say as you hurry to keep up with him. "I thought you were a wild animal."

"Some folks would agree with that," says Isaac, his eyes twinkling. "Like Aggie Ellison."

"Mrs. Ellison!" you say. "Is she okay? She was going to be robbed by two escaped prisoners!"

Turn to page 105.

"Grab hold!" you yell at the boy, thrusting your sapling toward him.

Eyes wide with fear, he grasps the end of the rod so quickly that you almost lose your footing.

"Stand still!" you command him. "Hold the rod firmly."

You wait what seems like many minutes—but is actually a few seconds—until he has steadied himself. Then very slowly and deliberately, you pull on the rod, hand over hand, at the same time cautiously rolling your log with your feet, closer and closer to the log on which the Indian boy is standing.

When the two logs bump gently together, the two of you stand shoulder to shoulder.

"The logs will steady each other side by side," you say. "And if we move in step, carrying this one sapling, we can reach the other side safely."

He nods, and together you pace your steps until you are within a few feet of solid ground. Then you stop.

"Take the sapling," you tell him, "and go beyond the place where the earth supports the logs. I will follow when you are safe."

He nods, and you see that his eyes are moist with tears. "Thank you, Cousin," he whispers.

Go on to the next page.

You watch apprehensively as he proceeds along the log. Clods of earth fall into the chasm when his feet touch firm ground. Once you see he is safe, you start inching your way across the last few treacherous feet, knowing the support has been weakened. It's doubly difficult without the sapling, and you raise your arms to balance yourself.

When you reach the end of the logs, you lunge across the earth supporting them and fall forward on the ground, exhausted.

Turn to page 97.

58

"Keep it down, Fred," says a man's voice. "You might as well take out an ad in the local paper to tell the cops where we are!"

"So who's to hear us in the middle of the forest?" Fred asks. "The police are still searching the Boston area." He sits on the cot, and the springs sag down and touch you.

"We need money," the other man says. "That store closes at six. I saw the sign in the window. At closing time we'll clean out the cash register. There's only one old lady in there, and she looks about ninety."

"Yeah, it's a piece of cake, Stan. We can get food too. Nobody's going to look for us here. I'm goin' to take a nap."

The bed creaks as Fred rolls over, and you suck in your breath.

"No naps!" Stan yells. The bed jerks up as he yanks Fred to his feet. "We're goin' to go find some wood for this stove. It gets cold here at night."

The door creaks behind them, and you roll out from under the bed. Fred and Stan must have escaped from prison! Should you get Jason, or go and warn the lady at the store?

Cautiously you peek out the window. Two men, dressed in blue coveralls, are disappearing into the forest.

If you go back to get Jason, turn to page 43.

If you go directly to the store, turn to page 75.

"We're going to Henry's cabin first," you say to Stan.

"Why?" he asks suspiciously. "Is this a trick? Henry could be back by now."

"Henry's spirit never left," you say, surprising even yourself. "I need to go there."

"The kid's loony," Fred mutters.

"Where's Henry?" Stan asks, shushing his partner.

"Nobody knows," you reply. "He disappeared a year ago."

"Why do you have to go to the cabin?" Stan asks.

"I need permission to go back to his tree," you say. "I can't go without it. It's a sacred tree! You heard what Mrs. Ellison said. *Death waits for you by Henry's tree.* Well, if you don't want to risk dying, we'll have to go to the cabin first."

You look at Fred. He's rolling his eyes. "The kid's got a screw loose," he mutters.

"Shut up," Stan says. "Okay," he continues, in a tone meant to humor you. "We'll go by the cabin first."

As the three of you hurry toward the cabin you try to remember what else Mrs. Ellison said. It was something about writing. *The writing's on the wall!* That was what she said. She must have meant the drawing of the tree. There's something on that wall that will help you, but what is it?

Fred's voice interrupts you. "Okay, kid, here we are. Go commune with the spirits." He shoves the cabin door open and pushes you inside.

Turn to page 95.

"Henry won't see us coming from this side," you say, leading Fred and Stan to a spot in a direct line of view from Jason's writing table.

As obviously as possible you dart in and out from behind trees, calling back that you see movement in the tower. You hope that by now Jason is looking for you. If Jason sees three people, he's going to know something's wrong—especially if he listened to the six o'clock news.

"Place looks deserted to me," Stan says. He grabs a rung and starts climbing. Fred follows, and you come along behind. Everything is working perfectly, providing Jason has seen you.

Stan reaches the top, pushes open the door, and finds himself facing two armed policemen. Behind them stand Jason and Agnes Ellison.

You're filled with enormous relief.

"Lucky for me that repairman came to fix my phone," Mrs. Ellison says later. "He knew I'd never close up in the middle of the day!"

"I think I'll stay home tomorrow and read," you say to Jason and Mrs. Ellison after the convicts have been taken away.

"I'm afraid that's not possible," Jason says. "There's still a missing cash drawer. And some wood that needs stacking."

You groan. "I can take care of the wood," you say, "but how am I going to know what tree the cash drawer is under?"

"Maybe you should visit Henry's tree and get the spirits to tell you," Jason suggests, grinning.

The pillow hits him square in the head.

The End

Smiling, you turn to reenter the forest. But your smile dies quickly as a searing pain in your head makes you stagger backward. The last thing you see is the painted face and body of a man standing by a pine tree, his bow raised.

He watches in silence as you fall into the gorge, the arrow still quivering from the socket of your right eye.

The next day searchers find your body impaled on the branch of a fallen tree.

"The victim died instantly," the doctor says later at the inquest. "The momentum of the falling body when it hit turned the branch into a lethal weapon. It pierced the right eye as surely as an arrow."

The End

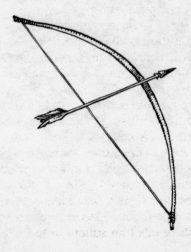

You sneak to the side of the building and pick up the shotgun. Pointing it in the air, you move slowly toward the store. But you forget about the unstacked wood. Your foot hits a log and you sprawl on the ground. The shotgun goes off like a cannon.

From your prone position you watch the men run out the door and disappear into the forest.

"Even some good things happen by accident," Mrs. Ellison says, frowning at you. "Now get yourself in here. They'll be back."

Sheepishly you go in as she marches out to retrieve the gun. Back inside she snaps out orders. "Push the magazine stand against the door! Pull the blinds! Then get down behind the counter and stay there until I tell you to come out."

You're on the floor reading a magazine when you hear a motor outside. It sounds like Jason's dirt bike. You crawl to the window and peek out. It's Jason's bike, but the convicts are riding it!

"Mrs. Ellison! They're back!" you whisper. "What'll we do?"

"Nothing," she says. "They've come for the money."

You watch as the men go to the woodpile.

"How did they know where to look?" you ask.

"I told them," she says. "Better they should take the money than wreck the store—and maybe us too."

You swallow hard. "But the money's not there. I hid it."

Mrs. Ellison frowns and says, "That wasn't helpful. Go open the damper in the fireplace."

Turn to page 45.

You're about to start back toward the ranger station when you hear a faint rustling in the brush to your right. You stare at the spot. The hot, humid night air hangs heavily over the forest, and your shirt is damp from perspiration.

Someone (Ben?) or something (a wolf?) is watching you from the bushes. Fear freezes you in place, and you strain to see what it could be, but the shrubbery is too dense.

You're hypnotized by the sense of another's presence. Should you run? Call out? Throw something?

Ben said the tree was inhabited by both good and evil spirits. If you only knew which tree it was, maybe some good spirit would help you get out of this place. You glance beyond the stunted pine to the other trees in the area. They're so tall that you can't see the tops. And their trunks are so big around that it would take several people with arms outstretched to encircle them.

The howls of the wolves grow faint. The pack seems to be moving to another ridge, and you no longer hear the cry for help. You shiver and direct your attention back to the brush. There is something over there, you're sure. Whatever it is, it will have to make the first move. You're not going to budge!

Your decision made, you sit quietly, watching the shadow of the small, misshapen tree in front of you as the moon sends silver fingers of light down through the stately pines around it.

That is where Jason finds you the next morning.

Turn to page 10.

You look to where the Indian boy is pointing. Two pine trees, trimmed of their bark, have been felled about ten feet apart, to span the deep gorge.

"We will start our journey across together," he says, smirking. "The one who first reaches the other side will follow our uncle as chief of the tribe." His eyes narrow as he stares at you. "We cannot both succeed this time," he continues, "for the earth on the other side will not support the crossing of two people. It will crumble when the first one reaches safety." He picks up two long cut saplings and hands you one.

He can't be serious! The stripped logs look like oiled glass in the watery light of dawn. Even with the sapling as a balancing rod you know you'll never make it across. But someone, something, some power, is forcing you ahead.

You stand poised at the head of one of the logs and look at your competitor. Your eyes lock.

"Now!" he says. As he speaks he holds the sapling chest-high and steps toward one of the logs.

"Wait!" you say to him, struggling to resist the force that is pushing you. "I'm not going across."

"Then take the coward's arrow in your right eye," he says, pointing across the gorge. "Have you forgotten? Our uncle's shaman waits and watches. His bow is ready to rid the tribe of sniveling dogs."

*If you choose to cross the gorge,
turn to page 69.*

*If you take your chances and refuse to cross,
turn to page 8.*

"Shut up, old lady," Stan says. He looks at you and Fred. "Go tie her up. I'll keep watch out here."

You take Mrs. Ellison back into the store.

Fred heads for the refrigerator. "I need food. You tie her up."

"A tourist might come by," you whisper to Mrs. Ellison.

She nods. "Go back to Henry's cabin first," she says as you tie her hands loosely behind her back. "Look at—"

"What are you two talking about?" Fred growls, hurrying over to inspect the rope around her wrists. "A baby could get out of this in thirty seconds!" He tightens the knots.

Then Fred shoves you out the door and steps back inside. He flips the sign in the window to CLOSED. Your heart sinks. There'll be no chance of a tourist finding Mrs. Ellison now.

"Let's go, kid," Stan says, giving you a shove. "You lead. And hurry up."

Your mind is full of questions. Is there really a fire alert? Is Mrs. Ellison trying to warn you away from the ridge? Or did she mean that, because there is an alert, the Forest Service will be patrolling that area? And why did she tell you to go to Henry's cabin first? What did she want you to look at? Maybe you can leave a clue there for Jason; he's sure to look for you. Or maybe you can lose the men in the forest.

If you decide to go to Henry's cabin first, turn to page 59.

If you go directly to the ridge, turn to page 84.

"I took a picture of Sarah," you tell Jason. "She was out by the water barrel."

"Give me the film," he says. "I'll send it on the bus. The prints will be back tomorrow."

That night, after a silent dinner, you try to apologize to Jason for snooping in his manuscript. And you try to convince him again that you're not making up the story about Sarah and Ben.

"We'll discuss it when your pictures come back," he growls.

The next afternoon Jason goes to pick up the pictures. When he gets back he looks angry.

"There's no girl in these photos!" he snaps, handing you the prints.

"This isn't possible!" you say as you stare at a picture of the charred ruins of the cabin. "The cabin wasn't burned out! And Sarah was right there by that water barrel. She gave me a drink with that dipper before I left."

Jason looks at you in alarm. "No," he says. "Oh, no!" He puts his hand to your forehead. "Come with me! We're going to town immediately. You may need medical care!"

"I'm not sick!" you protest. But Jason refuses to listen.

Your ride to town is less than fun on the back of the dirt bike. By the time Jason pulls into the driveway of a small hospital, you do feel sick. Jason puts a supporting arm around you and walks you into the emergency room. He speaks so quietly to the nurse on duty that you can't hear what he's saying.

Turn to page 40.

You look at the Indian boy and step hesitantly on the log, holding your balancing stick in front of you. You feel like a high-wire performer in a circus, but this is not for the amusement of an audience. It's life and death—your life, your death!

The log rolls threateningly under your feet as you inch your way out over the gorge. The Indian boy is ahead of you by several paces, and you fight to keep your footing on the slippery surface of the rolling log as you hurry to catch up. Only the person who reaches the other side first will live, for you know the weight of two bodies will crumble the earth supporting the logs. One of you is doomed to crash to the bottom of the chasm. You look down and try to quell your mounting fear.

Turn to page 71.

As you do you feel
something hit your legs.
Your opponent is using his
sapling as a whip! Holding it at an
angle, he swings again and again at
your legs. Your left foot plunges
frighteningly off the log as you
grope to regain your balance.
Your balancing rod jerks up into the air and
clouts the end of his, knocking it from his hand.
You watch, horrified, as he lunges forward to grasp
the sapling and loses his balance. His rod, now
held in one hand only, tips dangerously down on
one side, threatening to pull him off his log.

With a choked cry he lets go and the sapling
floats down into the depths of the gorge.

Turn to page 56.

Jason's snores fill the room. Cautiously you tip-toe around the screen. You quietly pick up some loose pages from the card table and tiptoe back to bed.

You dig out a flashlight from your suitcase and pick up a page to read at random.

"Sarah! Where's Ben?" The young girl dipping water from the barrel by the log cabin door hesitated a moment. Her long brown hair, tied with a blue ribbon that matched her dress, flounced as she turned to respond to Isaac's question.

Isaac! Isaac Cairns? You shuffle through the pages until you find the one with the sketch of the tree, and start reading.

He reached up and with a sharp rock cut off a piece of the bark—What a gyp! The first page ends here. Why didn't Jason finish it? Then you spot two words penciled at the bottom of the page: *Spirit possession.*

You lie back and stare at the ceiling. Is it a coincidence that Jason's writing about Isaac Cairns? Or does it have something to do with the Spirit Tree? Could Jason have found it? You set the pages down beside you. Is that why he's acting so strangely? Then a frightening thought occurs to you. Could Jason be possessed?

Jason's words come back to you.

"Forget the tree! It's dangerous!"

The sound of Jason preparing breakfast wakens you in the morning. As you sit up you realize the pages are still on the cot beside you. You stuff them under the blanket and pull on your jeans and shirt. You'll have to wait for a safe time to put them back.

Turn to page 30.

You prepare to spend the night under the tree. After brushing some loose pine needles into a pile, you lie down.

You're not sure how long you've slept when you suddenly awaken. A group of people are gathered in the clearing, and off to your left a bonfire is burning. At first you think it's the convicts, but you see six shadowy figures standing in a circle around you.

"It is time for the proof," a gruff voice says.

"Proof of what?" you ask as you are yanked to your feet.

"Proof that you are faithful to the tribe," the voice replies. "He who kills with herbs kills as surely as with fire."

"What are you talking about?" you say. "I didn't kill anyone!"

You're being mistaken for someone else! Has an evil spirit possessed you?

"You have the same choice as your victim," says the voice. "You can drink the cup or take the fire walk. If you live, you may return to the tribe."

"What?" you say. You look to where he is pointing and see that the bonfire has been raked into a path of burning coals.

"The fire walk—or this!" says the voice, thrusting a gourd toward you. Foul-smelling fumes rise from the cup.

*If you decide to take the fire walk,
turn to page 109.*

*If you decide to drink from the gourd,
turn to page 116.*

You open the cabin door and run all the way to the store.

Chipped gold lettering with black edges on the window says ELLISON'S STORE—MRS. AGNES ELLISON, PROP.

A tall thin lady with white hair stands behind the counter.

"Are you Mrs. Ellison?" you ask, entering quickly.

"Who wants to know?" she asks, turning to stare at you.

Stan was right. She looks about ninety.

"Call the police!" you say. "You're going to be robbed!"

Mrs. Ellison scowls. "I don't know you," she says.

"I'm staying with my uncle Jason at the lookout," you say.

"Oh, that writer fellow. Do you make up stories too?" She turns and starts dusting a shelf. "Don't know anybody in these parts who'd want to rob Agnes Ellison," she says.

"They're convicts escaped from prison in Boston!" you say.

Mrs. Ellison frowns. "Do you want a job?" she asks.

Turn to page 77.

"A job?" you repeat. It's as though she hasn't heard a word!

"A job," Mrs. Ellison says. "Work. I'll pay you five dollars to help me stack that cord of wood up against the building."

You look out the window at a heap of wood in the gravel driveway. "Look," you say. "Will you call the police? Those men are going to rob you at six o'clock. They want food and money."

"How do you know?" she asks skeptically.

You hesitate. "I went to find Henry," you say. "I wanted to ask him about the Spirit Tree, but he wasn't at home. They came into the shack and I hid under the bed."

Turn to page 19.

"Thanks, but I can't stay," you tell Ben, trying to sound casual. "But I'd like a drink of water before I go back."

Sarah scoops a dipperful from the barrel and hands it to you. The water is warm and stale but moistens your dry throat.

When you point the camera at Sarah this time, Ben does not object, and you snap her picture before you leave.

"Safe trip, stranger," Ben says.

You turn and hurry across the creek and up the slope. The moon follows you all the way back to the lookout. Jason is at his typewriter when you rush in the door.

"What did you mean when you said ghosts were living in the log cabin?" you demand.

"What's gotten into you?" he asks, slowly turning around. "You look like you've seen one."

"Two, I think," you say.

"What do you mean?" he asks, looking at you intently.

"I've just been to the log cabin. It's not burned out. It's inhabited. And I've got a picture to prove it."

"A picture of whom?" Jason asks.

"Sarah," you say. "Sarah Scott. Ben got pretty upset when I tried to take her picture. Until they decided that I was related to some preacher. They said the only visitors they'd had since their parents died were a preacher and a pack of wolves."

Go on to the next page.

Jason leans forward in his chair. "I warned you last night about reading my manuscript!" he says angrily.

"I looked at only a couple of pages," you protest.

"I don't believe you," he says, standing up. "I'm sending you home on the next bus. You can stay with your uncle Peter."

"I can prove what I'm telling you!" you blurt out.

Turn to page 68.

You grab the cash drawer and head toward the trees that back right up to the store. You wedge the drawer into the hollow at the base of a pine tree and spread dry brush over it. Then you run back to the woodpile and quickly rearrange the wood over the place where the cash drawer had been.

Mrs. Ellison comes out, props her shotgun up against the house, and starts helping you stack wood.

"What was Henry like?" you ask.

"Kept to himself," she says as she expertly stacks wood. "Got a letter once from the university at Augusta. Some professor wantin' to know about the Penobscot legends. Particularly about their Spirit Tree. Just like you."

"How do you know all this if he kept to himself?"

"Henry couldn't read," Mrs. Ellison says. "He asked me to read the letter to him."

"Did he answer the letter?" you ask excitedly.

"I wrote an answer for him. He told me what to say."

"What did he say? Does the tree exist? Where is it?"

"It exists," she snaps. She hands you a log. "Stack wood. I'm going in to make us some lunch."

Go on to the next page.

When Mrs. Ellison comes back with sandwiches and milk, you sit on the woodpile to eat.

"You actually shot a black bear?" you say, nodding toward the shotgun.

"Oh, that was a few years ago. Hot summer night. I couldn't sleep. Came out here and heard him crashing around. Good thing he was so noisy. I had time to get the gun."

"Why didn't you just go inside and stay there?" you ask.

Turn to page 85.

"Go back," you yell. "Fire! That tree's on fire!"

The men continue toward you.

"You can't fool us, kid!" Stan yells, shaking his fist. "We're going to get that money before we go anywhere!"

"There is no money!" you yell. "It's not there!"

But it's no use. They don't pay any attention.

"Look!" Fred yells at Stan. "It's the tree on the cabin wall!" Fred drops to the ground and starts sifting the dirt under the tree with his hands.

You cross the clearing and start down the other side of the ridge. Then you glance back. Just as you're about to turn away, the smoking tree bursts into flame. You watch as great licks of orange eat at its bare silhouette. In slow motion it gracefully leans to one side and slips into the stand of trees. Loud crackling fills the air as the flames creep into the summer-dry needles, igniting tree after tree until a half circle of red surrounds the clearing.

You sprint back toward the Spirit Tree. The men are running the other way.

"Get under the tree!" you yell. "You'll be safe there!"

Fred looks at you hesitantly, but Stan doesn't slow his pace.

"Come back!" you yell as you dive under the branches of the small pine. "Get under the tree! It's your only hope!"

You feel Fred's body thud down in the dirt beside you.

"I should've gone with Stan," Fred replies, gasping. "We're gonna get fried here."

Turn to page 31.

"Let's go," you say to Stan. "I don't want to be out there in the dark either." You avoid looking at Mrs. Ellison as you head out for the ridge. Jason will look for you at the store, not at the cabin. He knew you were going there to get his paper.

"What's so special about this tree?" Stan asks as you push your way through the underbrush. You tell him what you know about the legend of the Spirit Tree.

"Some fairy tale!" Stan says when you finish the story. A crack of thunder follows his words.

You look up through the trees at the sky, now menacingly black with an oncoming storm. Your haste to beat the evening darkness was useless. Already the forest is shadowy. The ridge is directly ahead of you, and the growth appears to be less dense. If you're going to lose Stan and Fred, now's the time to do it.

"Stay here," you tell them. "I'm going to check out a shortcut. If it's passable, we can beat the storm. If not, we're going to spend the night here."

"Nice try, kid," Stan says. "You must think we're pretty dumb. No way are you going to abandon us out here!"

"Then find the tree and the money by yourself," you say. You sit down on a fallen log.

"Let the kid go find the shortcut," Fred whispers to Stan. "We don't even know what to look for."

Stan hesitates. "Well, okay," he mumbles. "But no tricks." He looks at his watch. "You've got five minutes. If you aren't back by then, we'll come looking for you!"

Turn to page 49.

"'Cause he would have just followed me in!" Mrs. Ellison says. "A hungry bear isn't goin' to be stopped by a door."

"Did you kill him?" you ask.

"Didn't have to," she says. "Just shot down into that gravel, right about where you're standing. It sprayed up and sent him running. Limped when he ran off," she continues. "Henry says it sounded to him like Old Trois Pied."

"Who?"

"Old Trois Pied. Old Three Foot. A bear that attacked a French Canadian lumberjack forty-two years ago. The lumberjack dropped his ax on the bear's right front foot. Chopped half of it off. But not before the logger lost part of an arm."

"Forty-two years ago!" you say. "Bears don't live that long!"

"Maybe yes, maybe no. This is no ordinary bear. About every five years somebody spots Old Trois Pied. Smart animal. Knows how to survive." She picks up your empty plate and glass. "I'll take these in. You stack wood. I'll be right back." Leaving the shotgun outside, she disappears into the store.

Go on to the next page.

You stack logs for a long time. It's hot, and the job is boring, and you wonder what's taking Mrs. Ellison so long. Finally you decide to go and check. You climb the two sagging steps to the door and are about to enter when you hear voices.

"Just give us the money, lady, and we won't hurt you."

It's the convicts, and they have Mrs. Ellison prisoner inside!

*If you decide to get the shotgun and go in,
turn to page 63.*

*If you decide to get the cash drawer,
turn to page 25.*

"I'll stay," you tell Mrs. Ellison. You start out the door toward the pile of wood.

"Just a minute," she says. She walks to the cash register and pushes a key. An orange NO SALE sign pops up in the window, and the drawer slides open. Mrs. Ellison lifts out the tray of money and hands it to you. "Put this up against the building and pile the wood over it," she says.

"But what if you need to make change?" you ask.

"No customers today," she says. "It's River Race Day."

You grin as you take the tray outside and place it on the ground against the building. She might be old, but she's pretty smart, you decide.

You start stacking wood, then pause as a thought occurs to you. Maybe hiding the cash drawer isn't so smart after all. What if the convicts get angry when they can't find it? They might become violent. Maybe it would be wiser just to give them the money and let them escape.

You look in through the window. Mrs. Ellison has her back to you. Maybe you ought to take the cash drawer out of the woodpile and hide it somewhere else so you can just give it to them when they come. Would that make you an accessory to the crime?

If you take the cash drawer from the woodpile, turn to page 80.

If you leave it there, turn to page 3.

You lead Stan and Fred out the door and turn to the right.

"Don't try any tricks, kid," Stan says as you head into the forest. "Just take us to the money. No more mumbo jumbo about spirits and disappearing Indians."

"The truth is," you tell Stan, "Henry didn't disappear. He's alive and well and living in an abandoned ranger station not far from here."

"Whatever," Stan says. "I'm not the least bit interested in some old Indian. I want that money. It's getting dark and the wind is picking up. The word will be out on us by now. We'll be on every newscast on the East Coast. We've got to move on!"

"We're getting close," you tell him, looking for a tree that will serve your purpose. "You'll have your money soon."

You spot a small pine standing apart from some taller ones.

"That's it," you announce, pointing at it.

The two men push you aside and start scratching in the dirt.

"There's nothing here," Fred says. "Only bugs and stickers." He scowls at you as he picks a pine needle from his hand.

"Okay, where's the cash drawer?" Stan roars at you."

Go on to the next page.

"I suppose Henry came to his tree and found it," you say as calmly as possible. Your plan is working exactly as you'd hoped.

"Then we'll have to go and visit Henry," Stan snarls.

"Henry doesn't like visitors," you tell him. "He's likely to take a shot at us if he sees us coming."

"Then we'll be careful that he doesn't see us," Stan says.

"Right," you say. "This way." You start walking back toward the lookout!

Turn to page 60.

"I think I'll go to the meadow," you tell Jason. Your mind darts back to the paragraph you read about Isaac and a log cabin. Both the Spirit Tree and the log cabin are in Jason's book; maybe there's a connection.

"Be back before dark," Jason says.

"Right," you reply. "Does anyone live in the log cabin?"

"Only ghosts," Jason answers. "No one has lived there for a hundred years."

Hastily you fix some sandwiches and sling your camera around your neck. You say good-bye, but Jason is already bent over his typewriter, and he only grunts a reply.

You meander through the forest, stopping at times to snap a picture. You study the trees as you walk, but none look like Jason's sketch. Eventually the ground slopes away, and the woods open up to a small meadow with a narrow stream trickling through. In the far left corner is the log cabin. It doesn't look burned out to you. Red checked gingham curtains hang in the windows, and smoke rises lazily from the stone chimney.

You jog down the slope and jump across the stream. The cabin is directly ahead of you, and you stop to take a few shots of the structure.

"Don't be pointing that at me," a voice says.

A young girl, about sixteen, stands at a water barrel near the doorway. She's wearing a long faded blue dress, and her straight brown hair is pulled back from her face with a blue ribbon.

It's the scene from Jason's book!

Turn to page 34.

Mrs. Ellison's voice fills your mind: "About every five years somebody spots Old Trois Pied. Smart animal. Knows how to survive."

Of course! You change direction and follow the bear. Running, tripping, gasping for breath, you race ahead of the fire, wondering when—or if—you'll reach safety. You're almost ready to give in to your aching body and seared lungs when you stumble through a clump of blackberry bushes and almost fall into a stream. Hastily you look around for a float. Wrenching a rotted log from its mooring in the underbrush, you hug it like a pillow and fling yourself into the shallow water, kicking your way along the current until you are far downstream.

The next morning Jason and the rescue team find you on the bank, chilled and exhausted, but alive.

"Stan and Fred are on their way back to Boston," Jason tells you later, when you wake up. "It's a miracle they got out alive. We lost a lot of animals that got trapped below the ridge."

"It's a miracle that I got out alive too," you tell him. "If Mrs. Ellison hadn't told me about Old Trois Pied, I'd be dead. I was following the other animals. And to think I thought the bear was a threat!"

"The threats in our lives are often what save us," Jason says.

"Did you pick that up at the Spirit Tree?" you ask.

Jason just grins and turns back to his typewriter.

The End

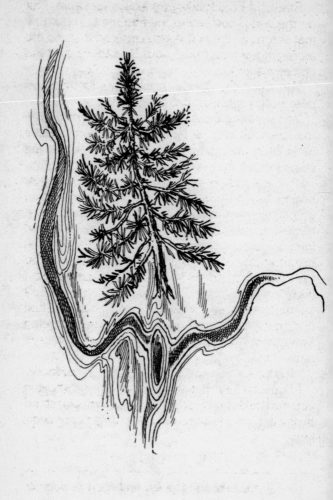

Stan and Fred follow you inside the cabin. "Sit on the bed," you say to the two men. You know that as long as they think you can lead them to the money, they won't hurt you. Besides, they think you're crazy.

You sit on the floor in front of the etching and raise your hands, muttering quietly.

You squint at the drawing, concentrating on the markings around the tree rather than on the tree itself. Stan and Fred whisper impatiently on the other side of the room.

You're about to give up on finding the clue you hoped would be there when a thought occurs to you. The wavy lines that end at a knothole at the base of the drawing could be trails to the tree! One long line comes in from the top left, a shorter one from the side on the right. The knothole must be the cabin! You could take them by one trail, escape, and come back by the other. They wouldn't know a second trail existed! It occurs to you that finding the tree is no longer as important as getting away from it is going to be. You mutter Henry's name twice and stand up.

"It is time," you say, trying to sound mysterious.

"You can say that again," says Fred, shoving you out the door. Ignoring his comment, you stand by the cabin for a moment, trying to get your bearings.

If you take the top left trail, turn to page 6.

If you take the trail to the right side, turn to page 90.

Stan grabs you and knocks you to the ground. "You've been lying to us! There's no cashbox here! You just wanted a chance to escape!" He holds a pocket knife just inches from your throat.

"No!" you gasp, struggling to get free. "I lied about the cashbox, but not about the tree. You heard Mrs. Ellison! Death waits at Henry's tree! And you picked a pinecone! I saw you!"

You struggle against his strength as the blade comes closer. Desperate, you clamp your teeth into his hand. With a roar his fingers open. You grab the knife, and as he wrestles to get it back, blood spurts from a slash on his wrist.

"I'll get you for this!" Stan roars.

Suddenly he is jerked to his feet from behind. "You fool!" Fred snaps. "Do you want to add murder to the list?" He turns to you. "Do you know first aid? Fix it so he stops bleeding."

Quickly you kick off your sneaker and remove a sock. "Sit down," you tell Stan. He's pale and trembling. As you bandage the cut he stares, dazed, at the pinecone in his other hand.

"That should stop it," you say, looking up.

But your voice drops as you look at the sky beyond the clearing. A rosy glow is flooding the horizon, and the smoke you thought you had imagined is real.

"Fire!" you yell at Fred. "Help me get Stan down the ridge!"

But Fred has already started down the slope. You pull Stan to his feet, leaning under his bulk. "Come on!" you say, angrily. "Walk!"

Turn to page 106.

The Indian boy is by your side in seconds.

"Why?" he demands. "Why did you send me first, when you knew the first one across would be chief? Why did you save my life?"

You look into his dark brown eyes and see a different person than the smirking competitor who tried to kill you out on the gorge. You feel different too. The force that was propelling you mysteriously disappeared at some point while you were walking the logs. Were you both possessed?

"I don't want to be chief of the tribe," you tell him. "And saving your life also saved mine. Alone out there, we both would have perished. Go to your people."

He sits on his haunches for a few moments, staring at you.

"If that is what you want, I will go," he says. "But I will take your wisdom with me. I thank you for my life."

He disappears into the trees and you struggle to get up. But emotional and physical stress have drained you. You fall back on the soft pine needles and sleep.

Turn to page 104.

You run blindly—crashing down the steep side of the ridge into dense forest. Fear of the men chasing you and fear of nature's fury give you speed that you had not thought possible. You look back once and see a wall of red washed across the twilight sky. Forked lightning crackles, and thunder like a hundred drums pounds in your ears.

Suddenly you are aware of the animals. Rabbits and gophers streak past you in the wake of the fire. Deer and porcupines and skunks risk proximity with a human, because of a greater threat. A loud crashing to your left makes you turn. It's not an explosion of flame as you expect, but a bear—a great black bear, rumbling out of the underbrush. Your heart throbs in your throat as you stop to let him pass. His finely tuned senses alert him to your presence, but he only glances at you, grunting as he passes, almost close enough to touch.

The bear moves steadily, not taking the same path as the other animals, but veering off to the left. And as he goes you notice that his gait is uneven—he limps. It's Old Trois Pied, the bear Mrs. Ellison faced at the store—the bear who mangled the logger!

Smoke fills your nostrils and lungs as you gasp for breath. You must move on—and quickly.

Heat from the blaze presses in on you, and sparks from the pine needles explode at your feet. You hesitate, unsure of which direction you should go. No place seems safe! Two deer race by, and you turn to follow, but go only a few paces and stop short.

Turn to page 93.

"But how do you know all this? How did Henry know?" you ask.

"Henry found them," Jason says.

"The preacher?" you ask.

Jason nods.

"But that's impossible! It happened one hundred years ago!"

"Henry had been to the tree," Jason explains. "While he was there, he"—Jason's voice cracks. "He was possessed by the spirit of the preacher. You see, the Indians believe the tree is a resting place for spirits—both good and evil. The spirits wait in its branches to take over a living body so they can return to earth and complete their work here. It happens infrequently—only at certain times of the moon or when the tree is violated in some way."

"What work did the preacher have to complete?" you ask.

"On his first visit he promised Ben and Sarah he would give their parents a decent burial. But he was afraid that he would contract cholera himself. So he left in the night."

"But Sarah said he *had* buried their parents!" you say.

Jason nods. "He did," he says, "one hundred years later. When he went back in Henry's body. And using Henry's body, he also went back and found the burned-out cabin."

"But what about the Ben and Sarah I saw?" you ask. "Unless . . . unless . . ." Your eyes widen with fear. "Do you think it was their spirits in the bodies of other people?"

Turn to page 115.

Heat envelops you as you race the length of the coals. When your feet finally pound down on the forest floor, searing pains race up through your legs. But you don't stop—at any moment you expect to hear your tormentors following. At last you sink to the ground, exhausted. The only sound in the night is your own labored breathing.

Jason and a rescue team find you there the next morning.

At the hospital the doctors are puzzled. "I don't understand it," says one doctor to Jason. "The blisters on the child's feet are more like burns than like those from excessive hiking. They aren't bad ones, but I suggest the patient go to the burn center in the city just to be safe."

You smile as you doze off. The city is going to look wonderful after your experience in the forest. You don't ever want to see another pine tree again.

The End

You don't care if the legend is just a story. It's a scary one, and you're getting out of this clearing! As you try to figure out which direction to take, a moaning sound erupts from high in the branches of the Spirit Tree. You freeze in place, looking up. A white light is dancing in the upper branches.

You force yourself to move away from the tree, but as you take a step a stabbing pain in your right foot makes you stumble. Something sharp is in your shoe. You sit down to remove the offending object, but when you reach for the laces, you realize you're not wearing your jogging shoes.

Your feet are protected by moccasins!

With trembling hands you slip off the moccasin. A piece of pine bark lies inside.

"No!" you say, horrified. "It's the legend coming to life!"

"Are you invoking the help of the spirits, Cousin?" asks a voice behind you.

You jump to your feet and turn around. You are facing an Indian boy about your own age.

"It is time for the test," he continues, pointing at the sky.

Over the horizon you can see the first thin rays of sunlight. It's dawn. But it can't be!

"Come," says the boy. He walks swiftly into the forest. You thrust your foot into the moccasin and follow him, desperately struggling with the force that is propelling you.

He stops at the edge of a deep gorge. "This crossing is the final test," he says. "We have been equally matched in the others."

Turn to page 65.

The rescue team finds you the next day.

"I can tell you what happened to the Indian boy who put the bark in his moccasin," you tell Jason when you're safely back at the tower.

When you finish telling him about your adventure, Jason puts his arm around you. "I'm so grateful that you're safe," he says. "Henry said the tree was dangerous. Now I believe him." He chuckles. "And thanks to you, I'll make my deadline. Tomorrow I'll write the ending."

About a year later you receive a package in the mail.

"It's Jason's new book," your mother says as you unwrap it.

"Not exactly," you say, pointing to the cover. "This one has two authors." There beneath Jason's name is your own.

The End

"Aggie's okay," says Isaac, grinning. "Them fellows will learn to be more choosy about who they're goin' to rob."

"I'm glad she's okay," you say, with a sigh of relief.

"She's fine, and the police are bringing them fellows back to Boston. It was Aggie who sent me after you."

"Thanks," you say. You hesitate for a minute and then continue. "I saw Henry back there. He offered to take me to the tree."

Isaac smiles. "Henry. Haven't seen him myself in five months or so." His voice drops. "I miss him. We used to spend a lot of time out here, hiking and fishing. . . ."

"How does he survive in the forest?" you ask.

"Same as you survive in your town," he replies. "This is his home. He knows every path in the forest."

"Well, I wish I knew at least one or two," you say, "so I wouldn't get lost. I don't want to spend the whole summer being rescued. Jason's too wrapped up in his book to go exploring with me."

Isaac looks at you carefully. "If Henry trusted you enough to offer to show you the tree," he says, "then you and I will get along just fine. Tell you what. You meet me at the store tomorrow morning at six-thirty, and we'll start some forest training. Most townfolk don't have no head for nature, but in your case it's going to be different."

The End

Stan looks at you blankly. "No use running," he mumbles. "I'm gonna die in a fire." He opens his fingers to expose the pinecone.

"That's no crystal ball!" you say, pulling him along. "I lied. I don't know if that's from Henry's tree. I've never been to Henry's tree!"

You grab Stan's arm and drag him down the slope, both of you coughing and sputtering in the smoke that's rolling after you. You've almost reached the bottom of the ridge when you hear the Forest Service helicopter overhead.

That night, safe inside the ranger station, you tell Jason about your adventures.

"You know, I couldn't convince Stan that I didn't know where Henry's tree was. It could have been that tree or any one of a hundred others. But he wouldn't listen. He just kept staring at that pinecone and saying he was going to die in a fire. He really believed that he knew what was going to happen to him."

Jason shrugs. "All of us believe what we want to believe," he says, snapping on the radio. "Let's get a fire report."

The announcer's voice fills the tower:

"Here's a bulletin: Stanley Mierte, one of the convicts rescued from the Wolf Ridge blaze this afternoon, escaped from custody tonight and has been killed in a fiery crash in a stolen car."

"Jason," you whisper, with a shiver. "Did I—"

Jason nods. "Yes, you did. You found Henry's tree."

The End

You brush the gourd aside and step toward the bed of glowing coals. You read somewhere that natives of Fiji walk on hot coals without getting burned. Maybe if you really concentrate, you can run the fire walk and escape these people. Suddenly two warriors grasp you from behind and lift you up, while another strips your running shoes from your feet.

"No!" you cry, struggling uselessly against them.

You look down at your bare feet, and back up to the solemn face of the leader. "Now," he says curtly, nodding to you.

The warriors are lined along both sides of the fire walk, bows raised, arrows pointed at you. You take a deep breath and sprint toward the glowing pathway. Ten strides should get you across.

Turn to page 101.

"We've got to stop them!" you whisper, nudging Mrs. Ellison.

"They'll stop each other," she whispers back.

"Here it is!" Fred yells, tugging at the drawer.

"Let me have it!" Stan shouts, pushing Fred aside.

"*I* found it!" Fred says, shoving him away.

Stan grabs a piece of wood and swings at Fred's head. Fred ducks and then tackles him. By the time the fight is over, both men are lying dazed and injured on top of the scattered wood.

"Now it's time for me to get the shotgun," Mrs. Ellison says, getting up. "You go to the lookout tower and have Jason radio for help. I'll watch them."

Within an hour the convicts are in custody.

"How did you know they were going to fight?" you ask Mrs. Ellison. "Are you psychic or something?"

"Human nature," she says, laughing. "Did you think I'd been to Henry's tree?"

"That's not funny," you grumble. "Tomorrow I'm going to find that tree. I'm right back where I started this morning."

Mrs. Ellison nods toward the scattered wood. "In more ways than one."

You groan. "That's not funny either," you say.

The End

"Do you think that Ben and Sarah were spirits?" you whisper to Jason. "Ghosts?"

"It's the only explanation I can think of," he replies.

"Would they have known about the Spirit Tree?"

"Probably. Their grandfather was a Penobscot."

"I don't think I want to find it anymore," you say.

Jason smiles. "I've stopped searching too."

"Is there anything more about Ben and Sarah in here?" you ask, tapping the cover of the history book.

"Some," he says. "I'm going to get back to the typewriter. Why don't you read for a while?"

You settle down with the book and read for a long time. Then you look at Jason's version. When you've finished the story about the Scott family, you hand the book back to Jason.

"I'm glad you changed the ending," you say to him.

"Me too," Jason replies, smiling.

In the real account of the Scotts the young stranger dies.

The End

Puzzled and curious, you get the page from the wastebasket.

The intruder slid under the cot and pulled the edge of the gray blanket down just as the door creaked open. "Keep it down, Fred!" The man's voice was gruff. "You might as well take out an ad in the local paper. . . ."

But Jason wrote that before you came back! You move quickly to throw your belongings into your suitcase. You arrive at the store just in time to catch the bus to the city. When you finally reach your mother by phone, she is sympathetic.

"Jason is strange," she agrees. "I'll wire your plane fare."

You spend a marvelous summer in France.

The End

The thunder seems twice as loud inside the covered bridge. Shivering, you crawl in farther to escape the rain that's pelting in through the entrance. Even with the wind gusting through the gorge the bridge seems steady and stable. With a sigh of relief you sit on the wooden floor and lean against the wall.

The bridge certainly seems safe enough. Jason must have been mistaken, or else he was lying, to keep you from going across. It's not even swaying! And the storm is subsiding. Now that you've come this far, you might as well cross to the other side and see if you can find the tree.

You rest a few moments and start moving down the length of the covered bridge. It's dark, and an occasional gust of wind whistles in through the cracks and startles you. You're relieved when you finally see daylight at the other end. The sudden storm has passed to another part of the forest.

As you approach the opening you see a rainbow framing a pine tree on the ridge above you. Your heart pounds in your throat. There's no mistaking that tree! It's exactly like Jason's sketch!

The Spirit Tree! You've found it! Jason lied. It does exist!

But Jason didn't lie about the bridge. You're still staring at the tree when the rockslide hits. You and the bridge plummet to the bottom of the gorge.

The End

Jason shrugs. "Maybe they had unfinished business too," he says. "I don't know. It's almost dawn. Let's go back to the meadow together."

You hardly talk at all as you retrace your steps. And when you get to the top of the ridge, you stare down at the scene in front of you, speechless. There, in the meadow, is the burned-out shell of a deserted log cabin—the same log cabin in which you ate supper just a few hours earlier.

"It's been that way for years," Jason says softly.

"Just a few hours ago Ben and Sarah were living there!" you say. "I didn't make them up! They were real! Real flesh-and-blood people! Not ghosts!"

"I believe you," he says, putting his arm around your shoulder. "Everything we experience is real, even if we can't explain it. Come on. Let's go home."

He turns to start back and then stops. "You're luckier than most people," he whispers, pointing. "You have proof."

You look down and bend over to pick up Benjamin's knife, gleaming in a bed of pine needles on the forest floor.

The End

You take the gourd and bring it to your lips, trying not to breathe the acrid fumes. What strange mixture of herbs does it contain? Is it poison?

You close your eyes and drink.

It takes three big swallows to empty the cup. Each time you raise it to your lips, the tribesmen moan mournfully in unison, as though counting.

On the last swallow you feel yourself growing weak. Your legs are unsteady, and your body trembles as you sink to the ground. The moaning stops, and when you open your eyes you're looking down on the clearing. It's as if you are floating in the air, hovering near the uppermost branches of the Spirit Tree.

There is no one near. The shadowy figures have disappeared. You settle on a branch to wait. You know it's only a matter of time until someone will come—someone whose body you can possess, so you can return to the world of mortals.

Rescue teams search for days. Your body is never found. But your spirit lives on in the branches of the Spirit Tree.

The End

ABOUT THE AUTHOR

LOUISE MUNRO FOLEY is the author of many books for young readers, including *The Lost Tribe, The Mystery of the Highland Crest, The Mystery of Echo Lodge,* and *Danger at Anchor Mine,* in the Choose Your Own Adventure series. She has also written a newspaper column, and her articles have appeared in the *Christian Science Monitor, The Horn Book,* and *Writer's Digest.* Ms. Foley has won several national awards for writing and editing. In addition to writing, she has hosted shows on radio and television in the United States and Canada. A native of Toronto, Ontario, Canada, Ms. Foley now lives in Sacramento, California. She has two sons.

ABOUT THE ILLUSTRATOR

RON WING is a cartoonist and illustrator who has contributed work to many publications. For the past several years, he has illustrated the Bantam humor series, Larry Wilde's Official Joke Books. In addition, he has illustrated *The Throne of Zeus, The Evil Wizard, Search for the Mountain Gorillas,* and *You Are a Shark,* in Bantam's Choose Your Own Adventure series. A graduate of Pratt Institute, Mr. Wing now lives and works in Benton, Pennsylvania, where he pursues his love of painting.

2/86